Mountain Man's Hideout

DEE ELLIS

Mountain Hideout by Dee Ellis
© 2020 by Dee Ellis. All rights reserved.
No part of this book may be reproduced in any written, electronic, recording, or photocopying without written permission of the publisher or author. The exception would be in the case of brief quotations embodied in the critical articles or reviews and pages where permission is specifically granted by the publisher or author.

Cover Design: Dee Ellis
Interior Formatting: Dee Ellis
Publisher: Hummingbird Press

Hi Reader!

I LOVE to hear from my readers so come find me and let's chat books, movies, music, and any old thing you fancy! I have a reader's group where I hang out and I hope you will too!

Find Dee:

Facebook: **Author Page**

Reader Group: **Dee's Dolls**

Instagram: @ **AuthorDeeEllis**

Twitter: @ **AuthorDeeEllis**

TikTok: **@authordeeellis**

Goodreads: **Dee Ellis Author**

BookBub: **Author Dee Ellis**

Website: **Dee Ellis Author**

Sign up for my **Newsletter**

Chapter One

Chapter Two

Chapter Three

Chapter Four

Chapter Five

Chapter Six

Chapter Seven

Chapter Eight

Chapter Nine

Chapter Ten

Epilogue

Driftwood Mountain Men Series

About the Author

More from the Author

Chapter One

Mack

"A hell of a storm is coming, no doubt about it," I grumble to no one as I peer toward the heavens.

The skies over my cabin are blue streaked with sunshine, but on the horizon, an awful storm front is clouding the skies. Across the valley, the mountain peaks are dusted with snow, but a lot more is coming. The firs bow in the heavy winds and the river between my mountain and the valley to the south is icy but churns beneath the surface.

Storms are coming and I for one like a good storm. It keeps me up on this mountain and away from most people. Keeps most people the hell away from me. It's exactly how I like it and just why I live and work on a mountain.

Five years ago, I wound up here in Driftwood after crisscrossing the country for a while. I was aimless after spending most of my life in the military. I had no one telling me what to do or how to do it, and it took some time for me to figure things out for myself.

Didn't take long to figure I don't like people much. Crowds and the big city are no place for me. After fifteen years crammed in tight spaces with a bunch of idiots—good men who I'd die for but idiots the lot of them—I needed space to breathe again.

Driftwood has plenty of space to breathe.

Settled at the base of a range of the Appalachian Mountains, only a few hundred people call it home. Most of those folks are blue-collar, good old boys through and through, hard workers who work the mountain. Logging and mining keep the little town alive and the back-breaking work and down-home spirit called to me when I passed through. I bought a few hundred acres on the mountain, built a cabin, and settled in to live my life my way.

When the old man who ran the logging in the area wanted to retire, I saw my opportunity. They needed a leader, and I spent my life leading. I bought him out and took over without a damn clue what I was doing. I've mostly figured it out, though. I enjoy the work, being out here in the middle of nowhere, working with my hands, and most the guys on the crew.

"You seem like a good man, Mack. No man, whether he thinks so or not, is an island," Bobby Dean is the bartender in the one watering hole in town, a smart man, and a pain in my ass.

He's not wrong about a lot, but he's wrong about that.

Despite ending up on a mountain as far from society as I can get, I grew up drowning in high society. My pop was a good man but a distant one who built a life our family never really wanted. We had everything we could ask for except for his love or understanding. Me joining the military enraged my pop and broke my mothers' heart and I never got to make up for either.

Burying them meant burying my past too. I never had plans to take over the shipping company or the fortune that came with. My place was in the marines, doing something that made sense to me. I never regrated giving it all up. Our old money never got me anything but time in prep schools, a few debutantes in my bed, and parents I barely knew.

"Ought to batten down the hatches for a few days, don't you think, Otto?" I call to the surly cat that sometimes call my cabin home.

All I get back is a bored mewl of disinterest. That'll do, I suppose. Taking my jacket and beanie off the hook by the door, I step into my boots. A run to town before a storm like the one I feel coming is probably a good idea. My freezer is stocked from a decent fall hunting season, but I need the basics. Some of these storms last for days up in the higher elevations.

"Anything I need to get you, you sour sonofabitch?" I ask him, bending to try to make eye contact with him.

He's a beautiful cat if I'm being honest, as far as cats go. A few months weeks after I finished the small two-room cabin, I came home to him sitting on the porch, like he was waiting for me. No clue where the furry gray guy came from, but I fed him some vittles, so he stuck around.

Sprawled on across the back of the chair closest to the fireplace, he stretches out, glancing up at me, as if considering my offer. He gives out a yawn and a long meow, as if deciding yes, he needs some goods. I reach out to brush a hand through his fur, grinning when he rewards me with a purr.

Guess we're one in the same—give us the right touch and we don't mind so much.

Light snow falls as I head out to my jeep, so I know I better get to town and back quick. Work is slow right now because we've had storms the past few weeks. I told the guys to take the next two weeks off and we'd make it up after the new year. Not because the holidays are coming since none of us have something celebrate or someone to celebrate with.

Hitting town in no time, I head for the main strip of stores at the edge of town. A general store, a mom-and-pop candy and sweets shop, a few small hardware stores, and some small shops fill the streets. As I head for the general store, I slow down when I notice a shop setting up on the corner.

Nourished by Nature. Huh. Sounds about out of place here as a place can sound. I come to a stop at the curb to get a good look inside. White shelving, windows with wildflowers and terrariums hanging from them, and rows of bottles and jars fill the small corner space. I don't remember it being there the last time I visited town, but it's been a bit.

Pulling across from it to park at the Mini Market, I take a moment longer to check the spot out. Last I recall, it was a candle shop that lasted about a year before closing. Not many folks can make a life out here and those who come here to start fresh often find it hard in the close-knit town.

Before I turn away from the soon-to-be-empty-again-store, I see movement. A figure comes out of the doorway, pausing in the small entry way. Bundled up in boots, a fur-trimmed jacket, and a stocking hat topped with more fur. It's all wildly out of place here and I stop to get a good look.

The figure steps out further into the gray light of late afternoon. At the same moment the cloudy skies part enough for a sliver of light to beam down just right. Backlit by the bright store with that sun shining down on her, I see the most stunning vision I ever set my sights on.

Lavender hair spills over her bright white and fur lined jacket beneath the stocking cap pulled down low over arched brows. Tipping her head back, she beams a sparkling smile up as the sun glows down on her, as if the two are old friends. The streets are empty besides the two of us but from across the road I hear her let out a laugh that flicks a switch inside me.

It's such a vibrant laugh that I find myself smiling for no damn reason.

As if she can sense that smile, she glances around then zones in on me. We're stand at opposite corners, facing one another, the only two souls out in here. Her head cocks to the side as she glances at me before her eyes circle the empty streets. Again, I want to smile but without any real reason.

"Hi, stranger," she shouts, lifting her hands to cup them so her words carry the fifteen feet between us, "I'm Mollie. This is my shop. I hope you come visit sometime! We open this weekend, just in time for Christmas. Bring your lady, your man, your friends, whoever!"

Now she gives me a reason to smile and I can't help it. I rub at my beard, as if I can rid myself of the shit-eating grin beneath it. In all my years I don't think someone's so robustly introduced themselves Never mind I don't have a lady—*or a man*—and few friends. Maybe I just found myself one?

"Call me Mack. Good luck with that, darlin'," I call back with a chuckle before I turn to head for the store, "you ought to get home, girlie. You see that storm coming our way? Not safe to be out in that kind of shit."

Mollie steps off the curb and crosses the street, careless of the snow she kicks up on her expensive looking boots or the road itself. Stopping a few feet from me, she cocks her head up at me, her eyes narrowing. I study her for a moment as she studies me right back.

Slowly her eyes narrow and I realize they're blue. But not any kind of blue I've ever seen. Turquoise I guess, maybe. Pretty, mighty damn pretty. But they flash with fire as her heart shaped mouth purses before she plants a hand at her hip and clears her throat, fixing her shoulders and planting her feet. Well, shit, I think I'm in for it.

"Darlin'? Guess it's a sight better than *girlie*. Now, just a minute ago, I told you my name. Mack. Hello, Mack. See how I used your name just now? Might try that when you address a woman, honey," she says everything rapid-fire, her eyes blazing as she takes a step with every bullet point.

"Pardon me," I stand tall when she stops too close for comfort but not close enough to touch, "Mollie. Nice to meet you. Now, get your ass home, wherever that is, so you stay safe. See you 'round, *darlin'*."

"Oh, you are adorable," she chastises me before that laugh fills the space between us and makes my chest tight, "you are so this place. The beard, the brute, the bluster. Dolled up in plaid and Carhart to boot. I love it. See you around, Mack. Maybe not in my shop, though, huh?"

She blows a mocking kiss at me before she turns on her boots. Unable to help myself, I let my eyes drop to her ass. In tight white leggings I get an eyeful and my hands itch to get a handful. I briefly wonder if she's bare beneath them or wearing a lacy thong. As those luscious globes bounce, I decide there's nothing but silky skin beneath those leggings.

It's been entirely too long since I've been with a woman. Years, in fact. I tried once I settled here in Driftwood, but it never worked out. Women tell me I'm closed off and I suppose they're right. I've got no room in my head or my heart to let someone sweet and feminine in. It ain't pretty in either place.

"You know what, Mollie," I say her name soft and low, liking how it feels and seeing her body respond to the sound, "I think I just might visit your shop actually. Might be first in line, in fact. Do like I said though, get your ass home before you regret it."

With a jerk of my head, as if I expect a woman that fiery to obey, I head to get the essentials and get home. That storm is coming and we both ought to get out of its way. Not to mention suddenly I very much want a cold shower and some alone time.

Chapter Two

Mollie

"What a tool. Like, an entire bag of tools. A tool *bag*," I mutter to myself as I watch the brute of man walk away from me.

I say it even as I watch the shape of his ass and the flex of powerful thighs in his worn in jeans. A flannel shirt and dirty boots fit him like a glove and that thick, dark beard makes it all even better. That is a *mountain man*.

Twenty seconds ago, I thought he was a god come down from on high. With snow falling and a storm whistling through the trees, today has felt ominous. Until we spotted each other at the same moment and the air filled with kismet. He offered me the first smile I've seen since I got to town two months ago. *Damn, what a smile, too.*

He seems no more friendly than the others, though. People aren't *unkind* they just...*are not* kind. In a town this size I didn't expect a welcome party. But I sure didn't expect to feel so out of place, either. Then again, I look the part of the city girl sweeping into foreign territory with her city-girl ways.

Truth be told, I grew up in a little town just like this one. A town that depended on the hard work of its community to keep it thriving. Too late I learned that community had grown tired decades before my time. I had to watch my home die a slow death before I could escape it.

That was a lifetime ago it feels like, but not so long I forgot. I left the mountains and backwoods of rural Georgia in my rearview to head to the bright lights of the big city. I took to the big city like a fish to water though. I loved the excitement of the unknown lurking behind every turn.

Too bad violence, hatred, and hopelessness lurked there too.

It took fifteen years to sour me on the unending despair of underpaid workers and overpriced living. I spent those fifteen years climbing a slippery ladder in marketing. I was good at my job, spotted trends quick, knew how to talk to the masses, and strived to elevate the brands I thought deserved it.

Five months ago, my efforts were not rewarded with a corner office and a view. My work focused on companies who needed eyes on their products to stay alive. I worked with sustainable brands; companies who took little from the earth but gave plenty back. They considered me a risk who put more weight on making good things than making good money.

"Too high a cost for you to be so altruistic," I recall the firm telling me as they bid me an adieu I never saw coming.

Being selfless and sparking hope cost me the life I knew. Losing everything caused me to lose myself for a while. My mother never raised quitters, so I knew I'd land on my feet. I allowed myself some time to mourn what could have been and then I packed it in and headed south.

Through my work I made connections with some good people. Those people—folks in branding, design, and product development—helped me find myself all over again. Creating something good is what inspired me. Both the city girl in me and the down-home girl I once was coming together made sense to me. I want to bring a little of the big city to a town like the one I had known but do it my way.

"From concept to counter in two months. It's impossible, Mollie."

"Nothing is impossible. We can source most of the materials from the location itself. Branding is paramount. Locals don't like outsiders coming looking for a quick cash grab. Most these folks can't afford luxuries or if they can, they don't buy into it. Our bottom line is to make sustainable luxury they will buy into. In the next three months."

Using everything I learned promoting businesses using raw materials, honest policies, and smart concepts, I created something of my own. It took a little longer than my goal of two months, but we managed it. Finding a well of amazing sources in Driftwood meant I was setting up shop in a town very much like the one I grew up in.

Much as I expected, so far, the locals had yet to buy in to the concept.

We open for business soon, so I need to fix that. I'm nearly finished setting up the little corner storefront that will be selling my brand of locally sourced, raw material self-care items. We will offer skincare items, essential oils, organic shampoos, soaps, and more.

Opening a shop in a town built on blue-collar, backbreaking work, is a long shot. Long shots payoff the biggest. I'm not here to make a buck off these hardworking people who don't know the difference between essential oils and motor oil. I'm here to source materials from them and pay well for those materials.

"You want to what now?" The mayor seemed shocked at my offer last week.

"To create my products, I need raw materials. Honey, mud, clay, spring water, biotic oils, and a dozen other items the folks in this town don't even realize I can source from them or their land. By source I mean partner with them and pay them well for, of course."

No word on whether a partnership with the town will be a go. My shop will open with or without their answer. Now I need to go to work on making these people like me so they will like my brand. That is a lot easier said than done, I'm learning.

That beautiful brute who just offended me gave me the first interaction resembling a conversation I've had that wasn't scheduled. I've been setting up shop for a while, but no one seems to notice. When I see townspeople, I smile and say hello, I shop at their stores, and I'm trying to find my place here.

"Get home, I said," a growl startles me from my introspection.

Turning towards that rumbly sound as heat rushes through me, I smile. He is gruff and rude but damn he's a good-looking man. Taller than some of the pine trees lining the tree and almost as wide, he is built like I always imagined a mountain man would be. He tugs at his thick beard and I wonder if it feels silky to the touch.

Dark eyes narrow on me before he jerks his head again. Big hands lift half a dozen sacks into the back of his jeep, a few at a time. Crossing the street because I never pass up a chance to chat someone up, I almost slip on the snowy cobblestone twice. Reaching him, I start to help him with his groceries, and he goes still, watching me with those dark penetrating eyes.

"The hell you doing, Mollie? You heard me; I know you did because you sassed me. I like that sass, darlin, but you ought to get home, wherever home is, because a hell of a storm is coming. Ain't safe to be out," he gruffs as he reaches over to take the sack from my hands.

Leaning against the open back door of the jeep, I peer into the bags. Two cartons of eggs, jug of milk, tons of veggies and fruits. I grin when is see the cookies on the top of the last bag. Oatmeal raisin. He may just be my soul mate. Who else loves oatmeal raisin cookies?

"Yes, I heard you. I'll be heading home once I finish up here. What's for dinner, handsome?" I cock my head at him as I ask.

"Steak. It's always what's for dinner for me, darlin. You always help strangers with their groceries?"

"Don't you? Besides, we *aren't* strangers, Mack," I wink at him as I finger-gun, sound affect included, "we just met remember? I'm Mollie Winters. Like the season. You are Mack. You are handsome but sexist. All women love the sexy lumberjack thing these days," I say with a smirk as I reach out, unable to help myself, and brush my fingertips over his beard.

I'm wildly attracted to him. I was the moment I saw him smiling at me in the snow. But a man is the last thing I need to worry about now. Let alone a man who seems to think little of women, based on how he keeps talking to me. Men think they're being kind when talk to us that way, I think. I don't want a stranger to call me darlin—he has to earn the right to that shit.

"Sexist? Because I told you to get your ass home to keep you safe? Or because I called you darlin'?"

As he talks, he's closing the door on the back of the jeep. This brings him close enough for me to smell him. Pine and fresh air and something woodsy. He lowers his voice when he says darlin' and my lady parts respond just as he means them to. I step closer too, reaching up to stroke his beard.

"Yes, those reasons," I manage to whisper as he moves even closer.

"Maybe I saw your ass and like it enough to want it safe? And maybe I never call women darlin' until I saw you, Mollie. Or maybe I'm a bearded brute who talks to women however I choose. Today ain't the day you find that out. Not with that storm coming. Either get home or I'm taking you home with me. I ain't leaving you out in this shit," he growls the words.

I thought I was attracted to all the mountain man shit I called him on before. Bossing me like a brute, the lumberjack look, that whole savage package. But it's much more than that and as I peer up into his eyes, I know I'm in trouble. They are coffee brown with golden flecks, and I could look into them for the rest of my life and see something new, I think.

"Do the women around here listen to you? Do you like giving orders?"

"I like it right now," he pushes closer, pinning me to the back of his jeep, "since you're asking. I don't talk to the women around here enough to notice if they listen. I don't give empty words, darlin'. That storm," he turns to glance over his shoulder, to the west, "is coming down on us and either you show me you're getting home safe or I'm throwing you in my jeep."

There is no doubt a storm is brewing right now. One that has nothing to do with the gray skies or the snowfall picking up fast around us. It's the heat that simmers as we stand here on this street, alone in the stillness. I feel my heart gallop in my chest as I reach out. Pressing my hand to his firm chest, I wait a moment. My eyes snap to his as I feel his beating the same rhythm.

"You wouldn't. We're strangers," I say as I tip my head back defiantly.

Before I can protest, I'm lifted off my feet and thrown over his shoulder. I should fight; kick my legs or call for help. Instead, I'm grinning as he throws the passenger door open to toss me inside. I wipe the smirk from my face when he reaches past me to snatch the buckle and belt me in.

"Guess I'm taking you home then, girlie," he says as the click of the belt punctuates his words.

I watch him round the front and climb in. With a quick grind of the gears, he throws it in reverse and speeds off. Away from the main road, past the house I'm renting, and towards the mountain. At any time, I can tell him to stop and let me out, and I know he will.

We just met and he looks burly and brutish and talks that way too. I've no time for this or for him. No time to have dinner or fun with a man. I have a shop to open and a town to win over. I have a fresh start to get going for myself.

I know without a doubt, though he has acted just as brutish as he looks, I'm in no danger with him. At least no danger of him taking me to the wilderness to hurt me. But he is head for the wilderness and a man like that could for sure hurt me. Just not with his hands or the ax I feel very certain he is skilled with.

All reasons for me to tell him to stop or take me home.

And yet, I stay quiet as we climb the mountain, heading right towards the storm.

Chapter Three

Mack

Outside an epic storm is brewing but in here it's more dangerous.

Throwing Mollie and her sassy ass into my jeep was a stupid move. I don't know what I was thinking bringing her to my cabin. I know a storm is coming and it might not be the one I was warning her about. When she gazed up to challenge me, I couldn't help myself.

Having her close, feeling her warmth, and smelling her sweet perfume in the jeep has my head messed up. I waited for her to challenge me again. Tell me to take her to her home or back to her shop. No protest ever came, even as we climbed higher and higher up the mountain.

Once we got here, she jumped out and I half expected her to take off running. I thought maybe she got some sense about her. But no, not this girl. She grabbed groceries from the back of the jeep and headed to the cabin. As if we've done this a hundred times before. When I let her in, still asking myself just I'm doing, she went to the kitchen to put things away.

Adding some wood to the fireplace, I watch her. As soon as we finished putting things away, Otto leapt up to greet her. He has never been kind to people, but it took minutes for her to have him purring and content. I mean, I can't blame him. Something about the woman has me feeling awful content with her here in my space.

I don't know what I was thinking bringing her here. Maybe I just wasn't ready to let her get away. I don't go to town often and the idea of not seeing her for a while didn't set right with me. I almost stopped and turned back a dozen times, but I had the storm as an excuse to keep going.

"When are you feeding me, handsome?" she calls from the kitchen.

That's at least the second time she's said something cute to me like that. I think she means it and it explains the heat at my face. Heat that has nothing to do with the roaring fire. I turn to answer her as and I have my answer why I brought her to my cabin.

The last sunlight of the late afternoon dapples her in warm light. Her eyes glow bright as they watch me. They spark with something bright, hopeful, effervescent. Everywhere I'm dark she is light and there is something about it that draws me into her. Clearing my throat, I stand and go to her, realizing I can't take my eyes off her.

With her coat gone, I can see I was right about her body. Lush. Full tits that look soft and round in her sweater, wide hips that flare from a little waist, and thick thighs make up her little frame. I want to find out if I was right and she's bare beneath those leggings. I can't, of course. She said it— we're strangers.

"You want to have dinner with me?" I ask finally as I sit at the counter facing her.

Smirking, she hops up on the end of the counter, leaning back so she's angled in front of me. Her long lavender hair is swept over one shoulder, but I can smell it. I want to bury my face in that thick hair and drown in that sweet floral scent. She reaches out, just like she did back in town, brushing her fingers through my beard.

Before it almost put me on my knees when she touched me. Now I close my eyes, leaning into the touch as a low sound vibrates in my chest. Her nails skim the side of my neck and then up the back of my neck. A shudder runs through me and my jeans get tight when her fist is suddenly tangled in the hair beneath my stocking hat.

"You mentioned steaks before you kidnapped me. I love myself some *meat*," she purrs, her fingers brushing through my hair.

My eyes flick open and she's right there, eyes locked on mine. I don't know what games she's up to, but I feel in the mood to play. I yank her off the counter and into my lap. Her little sound as she crashes into my chest has my cock aching as her ass settles against it.

"Figured you for a vegan, I suppose," I hold her waist, slipping my fingers beneath her little sweater, "but if you like meat, I can feed you, darlin'," I rock my hips and I see her pupils dilate when she feels me beneath her.

"Because of my shop I must be a snowflake feminist who won't eat meat or drink beers, is that what you figured?"

My mouth falls to her mouth as she sasses me again. It's plump and perfect and I know without a taste it's delicious. But I want that taste. I dip my head and trace the shape of her mouth with my tongue. Mollie lets out the sweetest, softest moan and I eat that sound up.

Claiming her mouth in a messy, wet, hungry kiss, I savor her sweetness. I taste her brightness and her warmth, and I'm starved for both. Her fingers are in my hair again, shoving the hat off my head. I shift her on my lap, letting her legs hang off the stool we're on as I fill my hands with her ass.

"Mack," she moans my name against my mouth, and I growl.

I drag her closer, settling her sex against me so she can feel what that sound does to me. I want to rip those sexy leggings off and bury myself inside her until this storm blows over. Can't think of a better way to be safe than wrapped up inside of her in this cabin.

"You want *some steak,* or you want some meat?" I ask as I grind my hips into her, feeling how hot she is for me.

"We're strangers," she says again even as she pushes her body against mine, shaking with need.

She's right, of course. I saw her in town and figured her for another passer-through. Someone here long enough to exploit us for profit until she bores of the pretty view. Maybe that's what she is and maybe it's not. But maybe I don't care either way.

I'm alone up here unless my crew has work to do on the mountain. I like it that way and I chose this life because of it. But suddenly, I see her there smiling into the snowfall and laughing like she thinks it's as beautiful as I do. As beautiful as she is. Suddenly I felt so lonely and I want her to help me chase that feeling away.

I don't know if it's *her* or if it's something more. It could have been anyone out there today, I guess. At least that's what I'm telling myself right now. That it's not *her*, just that it was *someone*. I don't want to feel this empty and this lonely tonight. I want to let this woman make me feel a little less empty while I fill her up for a little while.

"We don't need to stay strangers. No part of us wants to be strangers, you can feel that don't you?"

My hands are at the waistband of her leggings, peeling them down just an inch. Just enough to touch her skin. Her whimper as I press kisses down her throat vibrates against my mouth. I stand from the counter, her legs and arms clutching at me. I cross the room towards the fireplace, and we end up on the floor in front of it.

"Asked you a question, darlin. I need an answer. Do you want me inside you?"

Mollie arches off the floor, glowing in the firelight, moaning as she nods. Her arms lift over her head, her fingers clutching at the carpet we're laid out on. For a moment, I just look at her. I don't think I've ever seen something so beautiful and I want to remember every detail.

There haven't been many women in my life, and it's been years since the last one. Maybe that's what this is. Why it *feels* like this. Why my chest feels like a fist is wrapping around it tight. Or why I can't catch my breath when I look at her. Or when she looks at me.

"Never brought a woman to my cabin," I say, unsure why I need her to know this, "and I didn't kidnap you. I'd take you home right now, damn the storm. But I don't want to. Not tonight. Not yet," I whisper gently, making it clear I won't hurt her or demand something from her tonight.

Locking my eyes on hers, my fingers dip inside the waistband of her leggings. Slowly I peel them down her hips, never taking my eyes off her face. Until they edge past the juncture between her thighs. Her bare slit glistens in the firelight and I yank the pants away, making her gasp.

Dropping low, I breathe deep the sweet scent of her need. Eyes back on hers again, I kiss her pink flesh just as hungrily as I did her mouth. Her back arcs high as she cries out, her thighs spreading to make room for me.

Again, she waves her fingers in my hair, pulling, twisting, panting as I lick her, suckle, bite at her clit, and savor her.

"Oh my god," she whimpers as she twists her hips, feeding me her pussy, "don't stop. That's so good," she moans, lifting a little to watch me eat her.

I hook my arms beneath her thick thighs, locking her in place as I feast. She tastes like candy, but not too sugary sweet. Like peppermint maybe. I can't get enough of it on my tongue. When she comes, shouting with abandon, she feeds me plenty of that candy sweetness.

I lick her through the orgasm, but I'm not done with her. Once her shivers and shakes calm a little, I push her sweater out of my way. I barely wait for it to be gone before I pull at the lacy bra covering her and fasten my lips to her nipple.

My jeans are entirely too tight and rough against her silky skin. I reach down to fix that, but she beat me to it. Her hands swiftly undo my belt, the zipper, and then she's got her hands inside my jeans. I roar a growl that sounds more beast than man as she wraps her warm little hands around my stiff cock, stroking me slowly.

"Mollie," I whisper against her skin as she pushes at my shirt, seeming as needy for me as I am for her, "I brought you here to be safe. I swear I did," I bite at her shoulder, sucking, groaning as her hands guide me between her legs.

"I feel pretty safe with you, Mack," she says as she tips her head back, both of us going still.

It's a lie and we both know.

Nothing about this feels safe. Not how badly I need her right now. How badly it seems she needs me. It's not safe that I wish that storm would come and bury us in, so we never had to leave this cabin. It is dangerous that her laugh put the first real smile on my face in ages. That light and how I responded to is why we're here right now.

Sitting there by the fireplace, her creamy skin glowing and her eyes sparking hunger and want, this is what I want to remember. How my heart thunders in my chest and how when I press my palm over her breast, hers does too. I want to remember hearing our breathing over the fire crackling and wind whistling outside.

As I lie on her back and angle my hips between her thighs, our eyes meet and hold. My body bends over hers and we're sharing a breath as I push forward, touching my tip to her sticky folds. My eyes close as the first push of my hips settles me just inside her. Her little moan stirs a beast inside me that I've no idea how to calm.

"Wait," I say as I pull back, "Condoms. I didn't think of…I meant what I said about bringing women here. It doesn't happen so this *never* happens," I insist solemnly as regret starts to wash down on me.

"I meant what I said, too," she husks as her leg curls around my hip, tugging me into her, "I feel safe with you. Maybe I shouldn't, but I do. If you stop, I might just walk down this mountain in this blizzard, Mack," she teases with a smirk that sends heat rushing up my spine.

Dipping my head, I take her sassy mouth in a kiss as I push forward. I am wrapped in her heat, and it is fucking heaven. Sweet, soft, silky wet heaven. Her cries against my mouth as I fill her, the panting of her breath that rubs her nipples against my chest, the squeeze of her thighs at my hips, all pure heaven.

Lying her down, I hook my arms beneath her and thrust slow. I angle myself to hit that sweet spot. I know when I hit it good because she scores my back each time I do it. I like the hint of pain and I'll wear her marks like a memory. I bury my face in her neck and press my lips to her pulse, pumping faster, sinking deeper, harder.

"Mack...Mack, *please!*" she moans before she bites at my chest and I almost lose it.

Before I do, she arches off the floor as a sexy, raspy whine hums from the back of her throat. A smile twists her full lips and I feel like I've done my job by pleasing her. Now, for my turn. Shifting my hips, I sink my teeth into her as I start to pound into her.

I go still as my pleasure washes over me, coming so hard I can't hear the storm or feel the warmth of the fire. I only hear her, only feel her. For long moments I jerk inside her as I come, her heat going even vice tight as she comes again. She shudders in my arms as she whimpers sexy sounds.

"Mollie," I mumble for no reason but to say her name.

Shifting, I roll on the thick carpet so I can bring her astride me. I gather her close and watch the fire slowly die down. It will get cold if I let it go out, so I need to keep it going but I don't move. Not yet. I don't want to forget this moment, either.

I can't forget the moment I realize what a huge mistake I just made.

Chapter Four

Mollie

A rush of heat feels so different after being cold for so long.

That heat stings when it overtakes you. It's painful, almost. Uncomfortable for a little while as you adjust to it. Then you realize you enjoy the heat. In fact, you want it to be warmer. You want more of it. You would take this heat, whether it stings or is painful or uncomfortable or not, over the nothing of the cold you just left.

As I lie on the cool floor watching the fire die out, I feel that sting from the heat of what just happened. The heat of what keeps happening inside me. Little aftershocks vibrate through me still. When I woke up today, I saw the forecast and ignored it because I don't mind the cold weather. Now I think I ought to have kept my ass home.

"We need to keep that fire going, darlin'," his husky voice as he presses his hot mouth to my ear makes me ache between my legs.

His breath on my skin, the lazy draw of his fingers down my back, the feel of his firm chest beneath me, hell the smell of him. All the above make me ache. Not just between my legs, but it sure feels like it centers there. Or starts there at lease. Right now, he's not talking about another go together but the actual fire that's slowly fading.

Slowly I sit away from him, hating the loss I feel in his absence. It's a kind of cold that has nothing to do with the dying fire. It has everything to do with the warmth I felt the moment he smiled at me back in town. I wanted to grab hold of him and never let go because it was the first time in so long I felt hopeful again.

"Let me get it going then I'll get us fed," he mumbles, and I look away as he sits up to tend to the fire.

We're both bare, our clothes trickling in from the kitchen where this started. Really it started the minute he threw me into his jeep. I wanted him the second he smiled at me but when he touched me, I felt like I needed him. Now that I've had him, I expect that need to fade like the fire.

As I watch him stoke the flames, tossing in several more logs to get it going, it doesn't feel like it will. It's been a while for me, but I don't recall it ever feeling like this before. What we did it was...dangerous and careless but somehow it doesn't feel wrong. I've never gone home with a stranger.

We joked about it before but when I called him a stranger it didn't sit right. We are strangers, of course. I know his name, his cat's name, and nothing else. Only I feel as if I do. I learned things about him it often takes dates and text messages and flirting to figure out.

"Still want that steak, darlin'?" he asks as he stands to head towards the kitchen.

I watch his bare backside taut and flexing with dimples on each side with every step. Lord is he a beautiful man. He doesn't seem to mind me watching him strut around bare. At the small stove, he flicks the burner on before he turns back to me, waiting for an answer.

My eyes drop to the length between his legs. It's thick and wide and as I stare, it grows longer and harder. Being on my knees and pleasuring him suddenly sounds much more delicious than eating a steak. Flicking my eyes up, I see him watching me and I flush because he can see what I was thinking.

"Food first, girlie," he winks at me as he turns to the fridge, "you keep looking at me like that, I think we're just getting started here. Looks like we need our energy, don't we?" he teases as he turns back, slapping a huge steak onto the counter.

Pushing to my feet, I go to watch him work. I grab his flannel shirt and wrap it around me though that fire is keeping the place toasty. I bring the collar to my nose, breathing him in to my lungs with a smile. Sitting at the counter, I watch him oil the iron skillet, trim the steaks, and then chop up some fresh herbs.

"Tell me what you do besides cook like a chef, look like a lumberjack model, and do what you just did to me," I tick off his notable traits.

Facing me in all his glory he cocks his head as his brow furrows. Flushing, I flail a hand behind me towards the fireplace where he took me like a sweet savage. An impish grin overtakes his handsome face as he turns away, as if he's doubting the magic show he just put on.

"Never done *that* to someone before," he says, almost more to himself as he puts the steak in the sizzling pan, "so maybe it's you who just did that. But I don't *look like* a lumberjack, darlin'. I am one. I run a logging company here in Driftwood."

Taking a good look at him, I see it right away. His rough hands which felt amazing on my skin with his gentle touches. Big shoulders and thick arms from swinging an ax. He seems at ease here in the middle of nowhere.

Mack really is a sexy lumberjack mountain man.

"Well lucky me," I muse with a chuckle, watching him chop up some potatoes, "I just enjoyed a lot of women's' wet dream."

Making inappropriate comments when I get nervous is part of my DNA. Can't remember the last time I was so nervous, to be honest. I'm no social butterfly, but people don't make me anxious. It's a rare occurrence.

Being in close quarters with him and watching him make me dinner, I feel more anxious than I think I've ever felt. I'm not troubled by being up a mountain, naked with a stranger, or doing the things we just did. What has me so anxious is how right it feels, how effortless as we joke together, how simple it could be for this to become something that it can't.

No way am I falling for a sexy lumberjack right now. *No way.*

"Keep that sassy mouth up, darlin'," he says throatily, his hands planted on the counter in front of me as if he has to stop himself from reaching across the distance between us, "I'll be sure you enjoy a few more," he promises.

A shudder runs through me as his eyes travel over me sitting here in his shirt. Something shimmers in his eyes before he turns back to the stove. I want to ask him questions about his work, about this little town, and about why he's way up here all alone. But I don't think I want to hear his answers—too afraid they might charm me even more.

I lost everything this year and I want a chance to build something for myself again. I need to do it for me, and I want to do it without distractions. My eyes scan over his taut backside—that is one hell of a distraction.

He saunters through the little kitchen with such fluid poise, he is a vision to watch. Within a few moments he has prepped some delicious looking crispy potatoes, a perfectly cooked steak, and he pulls two beers out of the fridge to go with it all. Despite my earth girl business and mindset, I truly am a meat-and-potatoes kind of girl, so he gains points he doesn't need.

"Come sit with me, let me show you the view," he suggests as he passes me with the full plate in one hand and the beers in the other.

Following him through the main room, he leads me beneath the wide set of stairs. As we pass, I peer up to the second floor which seems like a large loft bedroom that takes up most of the upper half of the large cabin. Beneath the stairs he sits at a little nook overlooking the edge of the mountain.

My breath halts once I see what is spread out before me.

We're high up the mountain overlooking the town and the view the wrap around windows gives us is stunning. The cabin rests at the edge of a plateau just above a river that splits this mountain from the next. With the high peaks of the mountains dusted in sparkling snow, the icy water slowly rushing past, and the flurries coming down it's a scene unlike I've ever witnessed.

"Wow," I murmur as I take a seat beside him in the curved nook he's settled into, "how beautiful. I can see why you wouldn't want to leave this place," I muse as I bump him with my shoulder.

Beside me, he goes still for a moment, looking out over the view I'm sure he's seen countless times. He pulled on some sweats at some point but he's shirtless and I see marks I put on his skin sometime earlier and flush hot. As he turns to me to speak, something much warmer burns in me as I listen.

"I came through Driftwood almost by mistake. I was lost. Not on the road but lost in here," he taps his chest with a weary sigh, "I spent a lot of my life that way, I suppose. I came up here for a breather and I camped right here for a week or so. It was the first time I felt as if.... as if I knew where I was and where I belonged. Christ it sounds so corny to say it out loud, but I think I found myself on this mountain and I knew I didn't want to leave it."

"What were you doing before you came here?" I ask gently, unsure if whatever this is that's happening involves us opening up to one another.

"I spent fifteen years as a marine. Might've retired an old military man if I thought I could last that long. If I hadn't seen all the things I saw. Some military men go in with hopes of saving the world or seeing action. I just wanted an escape, I think. I'm thankful for it though, it taught me a lot, helped me find a good moral compass, and taught me how to work hard," he clears his throat as he looks away from me, back out over the view.

"Wow," I repeat, rolling my eyes at myself, "what do you think made you stop your journey here?"

As I ask, I lean into him, seeking his warmth, his touch, the smell of his skin. He lifts an arm to invite me in, and in I go, as if we've been here before. It seems to be so easy between us, this intimacy. I close my eyes as he talks, his fingertips tracing patterns on my bare thigh beneath the table.

"This right here," he says with a tilt of his head that I feel more than see, "I sat here on right where we are, in my tent, and I just felt peace. I hadn't felt stillness or peace in a long time. A damn long time. Maybe never. I came from a different world than here. I never wanted to go back but until I sat here, looking out at this, I didn't know what I did want."

"You built all this?" I wonder as I let my eyes circle the cabin

I note the handmade table we're at, the wide windows in front of us, and the huge stone fireplace. I twist a little to glance at the stairs with their wood and iron design and the kitchen with its granite counters and retro appliances. I like every inch of it and realizing he probably built it, chose every piece, and put it all together has that warmth blooming in my chest.

He says nothing but nods without a hint of arrogance but a beat of pride. Without a word about what I'm feeling—because I can't put it into words and right now, I shouldn't—I turn to him again. I brush my fingers over his thick beard, noting soft weariness in his mocha eyes, and the lines on his beautiful face. He is a mountain man, but a special one and I'm lucky to have met him, I'm sure of it.

Slowly I bend towards him, taking his full mouth in a deep kiss. He lets out a growl that vibrates from his chest, hooking an arm around my waist. I'm lifted onto his lap where I wrap myself around him. We kiss until I can't breathe or think and past me being able to feel anything but him.

When we take a breather, his eyes gaze up at me hungry and heated. He touches his nose to mine, passes his lips over my own, and then shifts me on his lap. We don't talk because I don't think either of us have the right words. How do you talk about this feeling coursing between us, trying to wrap around both of us? You can't really so we don't.

Once we do start to talk though, we don't stop. We talk about how he ended up here on this mountain and how he built the cabin. He asks how I found myself in Driftwood and about my business. We talk until words aren't enough. Somehow, we wind up in his big loft bed, after a quick tour of the cabin, and for a long time, we don't talk at all.

Late into the evening we share plenty more of ourselves but without words. We don't seem to need any words once we touch. In the warmth of his little cabin up on the mountain, I forget about everything else.

I even forget about the storm that brough us here because all I can focus on is the storm happening between the two of us.

Chapter Five

Mack

Early morning breaks too soon and I am not ready for the day to start.

Nestled naked in my bed is the most beautiful sight I've ever seen. Creamy fair skin and thick lavender locks against my black sheets is a view I won't ever forget. It's one of the many since I first laid eyes on Mollie that I've stored away somewhere safe.

Last night felt like it would never end. At the same time, I couldn't hold on to any of it tight enough to make it last. I took her again and again, aching with the need to stamp myself on her just as she's done to me. I won't soon forget the sounds she gave me as she came so lovely, the feel of her skin against mine as she climbed atop me in bed and took me inside her again, or the look in her eyes when we came together.

It was late when we finally ate the dinner I promised. She laughed and fed it to me as she snuggled naked in my lap. That was before we showered together, and I rode her body until I had to carry her to bed. I turn greedy and savage with her, things I've never been with someone before.

Other women, it might turn them away, but not her. No, my need for her just spurs her need for me. She pushes for more, harder, rougher, pleading with me to take her over and over. Before she fell asleep, she muttered something about me locking her up in my cabin and keeping her.

Truth is—in the past few hours that's exactly what's on my mind.

Bringing her up here might have been a bad idea but I feel like letting her leave would be the biggest mistake of my life. I can't get enough of her and I'm not ready to give her up. I've never felt like this before and I don't want this to stop just yet. Even if I know soon enough, she'll leave this mountain and likely never look back.

Lucky for me we aren't going anywhere anytime soon.

"Morning handsome," her smoky morning voice draws my eyes from the windows to the bed.

"Morning darlin'," I husk as I turn back to her, a coffee in my hand, "afraid I might have some bad news for you," I explain, waiting for her to take a sip of the black coffee, laughing when she winces just a bit.

"Don't tell me, you have no sugar in this shack," she laughs and sits up to stretch, letting the thick blankets fall away from her.

I can't take enough of the view in at once. With the windows behind the bed framing her just right, the mountains beyond, and the snowdrifts all around it is a stunning view indeed. I can't keep her here even if it feels like she belongs right there on this mountain, in the cabin, and in my bed.

"Don't need it with you here, sweets." I shoot with a wink at her as I clear my throat, looking away so I can get this said. "I knew a storm was coming so I thought we ought to get somewhere safe. I can't lie and say the idea of getting you alone up here didn't factor into what I did yesterday. But I mean it when I say I didn't intend to kidnap you or trap you here."

I start to pace a little and the cool hardwood keeps me centered. I can't turn this into something it's not. We wanted each other and we had each other. I belong up here on this mountain and she, well, she sure as hell doesn't deserve a life hidden away up here. I never brought a woman up here, so I never had to think about what comes after doing something so bone headed.

Yesterday I didn't give her a choice about ending up here. Not just because I wanted to be sure she was safe. I meant that, of course. But after I saw her in town, I just couldn't walk away without hearing her laugh again, finding out how she tasted, and what she sounded like as I took her.

After my speech, she sits up on her knees, reaching out to me. Her fingers comb through my beard trail up to tangle in my hair. When she touches me, it feels as if a switch inside me turns on. It's not just about wanting her beneath me or wrapped around me. It's about the connection I feel the minute her hands or lips are on mine—and I can't get enough of it.

"When you hauled me over your shoulder to throw me in that jeep, I knew I could tell you to drop me home and you would. I don't know how I knew, but I did," her voice is gentle, as if she's soothing a scared animal, "and I knew last night at any time, if I said stop, you would. It kind of feels as if we're not really strangers at all, doesn't it?"

Her big eyes are earnest, trusting, softened with want and willingness and I almost push her back into the bed. I want to take her and keep taking her until she can't deny that she is mine. Once I had her, I became hers. But I can't give her the life she spent last night telling me she wants. I don't even know if I want to try.

That's a lie—I want to give her anything. Everything.

"No, darlin', we don't feel like strangers at all. Good thing because right now, you might be stuck with me for a bit longer than I planned. The storm hasn't let up just yet, but it put a few feet of snow and lots of damage between us and town."

I go to her as I tell her the truth: we're stuck here in this cabin for now. Her big soft eyes dart past me, around the little cabin and beyond, then swing back to mine. Now those eyes darken with fear, and it guts me. I should never have forced her up here, but she made me act a damn fool.

"You mean…. we're...stuck here?"

"Afraid so," I kneel on the bed, easing her back as I answer her gently, now the one approaching cautiously, "lots of felled trees will take a few days at least to clear away. My crew will start clearing the roads as soon as they clear town," I soften my voice as I lower my head, trying to catch her darting gaze.

"A *few days* at least? My shop is supposed to open soon, I have too much to get done to be stuck here on this mountain for a *few days*," her voice skips a few octaves between morning sexy to tightly panicked.

"Mollie, nothing and no one in town is getting a damn thing done. Even the general store won't be open at a time like this. I tried to warn you it was one hell of a storm," I explain as I reach out to touch her again.

Her eyes narrow on me as she backs away and pulls the sheets over her beautiful body. I thought her fear gutted me but this, this slices me open. Her retreat. Her shut down. Turning her head, she lets out a weary sigh as if she has tired of the ruse we were living in since last night.

"Tried to warn me…yes, you did, I suppose," her voice is dull and cold, and I pull back from her completely, "excuse me, I need a moment."

Pushing the sheets away, she climbs from the bed, careful not to touch me at all. She takes the shirt she stole from me last night and wraps it tight around herself, turning away to head towards the bathroom. When the door slams behind her, I feel my heart sink in my chest.

Instead of torturing us both and waiting for her moment to end, I head down to the kitchen. I start a fresh pot of coffee because I know we're going to need it and pull out an iron skillet to make breakfast. Otto hops up on the countertop to glare at me for ruining things so soon.

Just as I'm filling plates with eggs and some bacon, I hear her footsteps behind me. For a moment, I close my eyes and imagine this is my life. This woman coming to join me in the kitchen before I head out to the landing to work. I imagine feeding her breakfast in bed before running late because I have to make love to her one more time.

It's beautiful but it's not my life and it won't be.

"Care to explain what *"a bit longer than I planned"* means to you, lumberjack? You swore you don't bring women here but maybe this is something you do so often it involves *plans*," her voice is accusing.

Turning to her, I almost drop the breakfast I prepared. She showered upstairs because her hair is wet and gathered atop her head. She also went through my things—which fills me with a weird warmth I can't explain—and is wearing a tank top tied at the waist, fresh sweatpants rolled up at the knees and down at the waist, and the same shirt she stole last night.

Not only is she gorgeous but she looks like she's *mine*.

I am on every inch of her. From the clothes on her body, to the marks at her skin from my mouth and my touch to the anger in her bright eyes, and the soap scenting her hair. It's all mine and looking at her, I feel like she is too. I like how it looks on her so much, I can't help but grin.

"Look at you," I say as I cross the kitchen towards her.

For a flash, she softens, cocking her head and inviting me in with her eyes. Once I'm close enough to touch her, that softness is gone. Moving to evade me, she sits at the counter and lets out a huff that I ignored her loaded questions. *Damn she's adorable.*

"Answer the questions, lumberjack," she grunts, reaching out to snatch a piece of bacon from her plate.

Sitting beside her, I hook a leg around her chair and pull it so she's closer. It brings her knees between mine and I close my own to trap her. I watch her chew her food as I slip my hands up her waist, making her face me. I bite back the smirk that her body's response—arching towards me, nipples budding up, heavy breathing—gives to my touch.

"I built this cabin five years ago. While it was being built, I stayed in a tent or in town during storms like this one. Take a guess as to why I built a cabin up here, far from town, and in a remote as fuck location? I don't much like people, darlin'. I prefer life up here alone," I say it and wince because since she's been here that's not the whole truth.

Swallowing slowly, she watches me with a look I can't figure out. I flinch when she reaches out, brushing the back of her hand up my face. I catch it, flipping the palm up and pressing it to my mouth. We share a sad sigh because maybe we both know this could never work. Whatever *this* is.

"You are evasive. I asked a direct question," she reminds me as she leans into my space, stealing a piece of my bacon, "what were your plans?"

Christ, I like her. I like the dip and curves of her body but also the way her hair flows down her back. I like the freckles on her face. I like how her nose scrunches when she asks me questions. I like that she bothers to ask me questions and cares about the answers.

"My plan? To get you to myself. I saw you smiling in the snow and I wanted to get you to myself. You called me a bearded brute, but you made me feel like one. I did care that you were safe and that don't make much sense because we were strangers, right? But I did. I was panicked that you wouldn't listen. I needed you to be safe and I wanted it to be with me. That was my plan," I say with another sigh as I steal a piece of her bacon.

"Well, you got me to yourself. You had your way with me for an entire night. Now it looks like you have a few more nights. What is your plan now?"

My heart answers before my head can.

I want to make her want to stay. I want to make her want me and need me so badly leaving this cabin isn't even a choice for her. As she gazes up at me with that fear and anger melting away, I know that I want her. I haven't wanted much for myself in a long time. Besides the open air and wide spaces here and a little bit of peace.

Without a doubt this woman will not give me peace.

What she will give me is the same joy she's given me since I first saw her smiling in the snow. She will give me attitude. She will give me sass with that sexy mouth. And she will give me pleasure unlike any I've felt before. I know all of this because she's given me all that and more.

What I don't know is if I can be something worthy of her. I work and I exist and not much else. I haven't had a reason to be happy or want more in a very long time. Getting by has been good enough but it has felt damn empty. That doesn't mean I know if the alternative is possible for me.

"I haven't thought that far ahead yet," I say softly, holding her little hand in both of mine.

"I think your plan was to make me *want* to be held captive up here in your little hideout. To get me and keep me to yourself. How far-off base am I, lumberjack?"

Her head cocks at me as she asks, and I see the twitch of her mouth. She is teasing me but she's not far off at all. I can't tell her that because it's crazy. And I don't think I even knew what I wanted until I got her back here. I just knew I couldn't walk away from her in town.

Now I don't know if I can let her walk away at all.

Chapter Six

Mollie

Christmas has a way of reminding you what truly matters.

For a long time, I spent the season catering to big city grinches clueless about how to celebrate the season. Flooding the shops and streets, overspending, and flaunting their wealth soured me on the spirit of the holiday.

Twinkling lights and merry sounds do not make a holiday.

Driftwood feels like a slice right out of a holiday tale. It is one of the reasons I wanted to open my shop here. To find joy and light again in a place I could call home. People in town have not yet welcomed me, sure, but I figured in time, and once people realized I came here for the right reasons, I would find my place.

I don't know where my place is yet—but I know the place I'm in now feels pretty damn good.

Mack telling me I'm stuck here with him both terrifies and thrills me. Since we got to his cabin last night, I've imagined just such a fate. Being locked away on this mountain with this sweet, sexy, sensual man is the best gift I could get this season.

It was not the gift I hoped for—that was my shop, and I don't see a way to make that a reality now.

"Christmas is less than a week away," I sigh sadly as I gaze past him out to the falling snow keeping us locked away up here, "And my shop won't be open for it. Maybe it won't open at all."

"Yes, it will," he says gently, coming to cup my face in his big, rough hands, "as soon as we can get back to town, I'll help. Hell, my boys will help. Whatever you need. I didn't mean to cost you that, darlin'."

His big, beautiful eyes are so earnest and gentle as they seek mine out. I move into his warmth, touched by the promise I know he means. I came here to start fresh, and I thought that meant the shop. Making a home in this little town that reminded me so much of where I grew up.

Going back there was not an option so I thought I found the next best thing. Come here, do some good, give back to the townspeople and make something for myself. I was so certain I had to open that shop to prove to myself I was not a failure.

Maybe I don't need that shop to prove I found my place.

"Admit it," I smile up at him as I tease, "you knew once you got me up here, we would get stuck here. You had to know. You told me last night you can sense how bad a storm is going to get up here."

His handsome face splits into a grin as he bounces his shoulder in a shrug. I laugh and lean forward, biting his bare shoulder playfully. He lets out a growl and bends to wrap his arms around my thighs. He tosses me over his shoulder just like he did before he secured me in his jeep.

He starts for the stairs, taking them two at a time in his rush. I laugh before I'm swung backward, my back hitting the bed. He's not even out of breath. My breath is strangled in my chest as he towers over me, gazing down at me with hungry eyes.

"I wanted you here, in my *hideout*," he teases me with my own words, "yes, I won't deny it. Never wanted anything like I wanted you the second I saw you smiling. I ought to have considered you before I brought you here. I didn't think about what it might cost you. I should have, Mollie, and for that I'm damn sorry. If I had known that storm would have locked us up in here…. hell, I don't know if I would have stopped, but I should have," he says with regret in his voice as he starts to step back from me.

"Do you mean it," I say so soft I don't know if he can hear me, "when you said you never bring people here?"

Last night, as he took me on a tour of his beautiful cabin and explained how he built every bit of it, I was in awe. Not just of him, but of his work. It's a beautiful cabin and while it is in the middle of nowhere, it feels very much like a home.

I hate the idea of him giving him someone else that same tour. I hate the idea of him touching the stone countertops and kissing them like he did me. Or showing someone how to work his massive fireplace before they snuggled up like we did last night. It's irrational and no other man has made me feel so…possessive before in my life.

"Course I did, darlin," he husks as if he knows what the words mean to me, "I never wanted someone in my space. Some of my crew have been to the cabin, but no one has ever been inside it. No one has gotten the *Mountain Hideout* tour, that's for damn sure," he says gruffly.

My face cracks in a wide smile I try to hide with my hands. His voice gets rough and his words harsh when he says something he feels. I like that. I like that when he says something he feels deeply, he looks right at me, as if he wants me to see the truth in his eyes. Now, he is gazing at me with something soft burning in his eyes.

"You don't mind me in your space," I say softly as I reach for him, needing the connection I feel whenever we touch.

He takes my hands and brings them to his bare abdomen, the tanned skin hot beneath my touch. His eyes flutter closed, his head tipping back. I walk my hands up his front, splaying my fingers out over his chest. He takes a shaky breath and I close my eyes, leaning up to press my lips to his ribcage.

"I like you in my space. It makes no damn sense, Mollie," he admits gently as he combs his fingers through my hair, tangling them to tip my head back, "I liked my life just how it was just a day ago. Just me and my damn self up on this mountain, felling trees, getting by. Now…" he sighs as he trails off, lowering to touch his forehead to mine.

"I came here to find a fresh start. To do something for me. I thought for sure that something would be that shop. But now…" I let out my own sigh as I copy his speech, trailing off as I gaze up into his eyes.

Something significant passes between us as we watch each other in the sunlight of early morning.

We might be stuck here because of the storm—but I feel as if the storm brewing between us has more to do with it than the snowstorm. I might not get my shop open before Christmas, but I will get it open. And maybe the folks in town haven't welcomed me yet—but this man has. If we are stuck in this cabin on this mountain for a while, I don't mind at all.

I will make the best of it while we're locked away together.

Slowly, watching his eyes, I slide my hands back down his front again. I take in everything. The way his skin smells, the way it feels taut and warm beneath my touch, the sharp intake of his breath whenever I touch him. I watch his eyes as I trace one flat nipple with my finger, then walk a single fingertip down his rippled abdomen.

Hooking my fingertip in the drawstring waist of his gray sweatpants, I give a yank. They come loose from his trim hips then fall slowly. His shaft pops out bare, hard, and thick. Between my legs aches at the sight of it and I wonder if I'll ever get enough of that thickness filling me.

"Still hungry, darlin'?" he asks in a rusty voice that sends a shudder through me.

Sliding backwards on his big bed, I turn onto my belly. He lets out a growl when I pop my mouth open, reach a hand out to wrap it around him, and draw him close. I dart my tongue out to taste his saltiness, humming against him as the sticky tip coats my tongue.

"Christ, Mollie," he rasps as I swirl my tongue around his shaft, as if toying with a lollipop.

Locking my gaze on his, I open my mouth around the head, closing it with a throaty moan. He growls and punches his hips forward, going so deep he nearly chokes me. I swallow hard as I struggle with his size, stroking what I can't fit in my mouth. I never tried very hard at this before, but I like seeing him lose control because of me.

He pumps his hips slowly, hissing when I suck and slurp noisily, still working him with my hand. Saliva coats him and drips from my mouth because I'm making a mess. He doesn't seem to mind. In fact, as it drops down his sac, he seems to lose control, fist gathering my hair at the nape of my head as his whole body goes tense.

I feel it coursing through him, his orgasm just out of reach. I suck harder, pump my fist faster, swirl my tongue and hum against him. I want to please him; I want to see it overtake him. I almost get him there before he yanks my head back roughly.

"Not just yet, darlin'," he grunts, slapping my ass so hard it stings, "as much as seeing you in my clothes turns me on, take everything off. No, leave the shirt on," he orders, stepping out of my reach, his big hand wrapping around his big cock.

Sitting up on the bed, I hastily obey. I kick off the sweats I pulled from his drawers earlier but leave the tank top on. My thighs shake as I sit back on the bed as he watches me. He strokes himself with one hand, reaching out to forces my knees open with the other.

"Let me see you. Does sucking my cock make you wet?" he says it like a question but we both know the answer.

His blunt fingertips swipe between my thighs, and I cry out. His thumb finds my clit, circling slow and rough, showing no mercy to the tender nub. I fist the sheets beneath me, my hips twisting to chase that touch. As he touches me, his fist pumps his length and it's enough to make me come.

He drops both his hands to my thighs, pushing them wide open, and I whimper. My head falls back but before I can beg him, his mouth is covering my sex. He suckles at my wetness loudly and I swear I can feel that mouth of his smiling smugly.

I close my thighs around his head, rocking against his tongue as he licks me, spearing his tongue into me. Fisting his hair, I buck wildly, my skin damp as I tremble beneath him. He bites my clit, his hands pinning me to the bed as I lift up, shouting as I come hard.

"Mack!"

As I shudder with the waves of pleasure crashing down on me, he bites my thigh. As if marking me. I reach out for him, eyes closed, senses in chaos. He's there though, crawling over me, his knees nudging mine up and out. I feel the press of him at my center and I hum, moan, cry out, and plead but he chuckles and pulls back.

"Look at me," he orders again, his voice commanding me to obey, "I touched you and I tasted you and took you. I want to have you, Mollie. I do want to keep you. It doesn't make sense and I know I can't. Let me have you for now, while I can, but look at me when you let me have you. I don't ever want to forget how good it is to be inside you," he rasps before he reaches out, ripping his tank top down the front a little.

His big body curves over mine, his soft lips kissing mine until I can't breathe. Then his mouth is everywhere, biting at me, kissing at my skin, marking every inch he bares. His teeth tug at my nipple and I arch to the abrasive rasp of his beard on my skin. Finding my hands, he pins them above my head, a big hand wrapped around both my wrists, and angles his hips between my thighs.

Plunging deep inside me, he fills me up until it aches. Until I don't think I can take it another second. And then I don't want it to ever stop. I want to always be filled with him, pinned down by his weight, trapped by his big hands. I wriggle to get closer, and my nipples scrape against his chest and it sends a zing of heat between my legs.

"Greedy little thing," he pants as he thrusts into me harder, faster, deeper, his words hot at my mouth, "can't get enough of me inside you. Just like me, yeah? I never thought it could feel like this. Is it just me?"

As he goes still inside me, I can only shake my head to answer. Because no, it's not just him. I thought I felt it when he smiled at me back in town. I could brush that off as the spark of someone being kind to me. When he told me to get safe and I knew he meant it, I knew it was more than that. And when he threw me over his shoulder and brought me home, I knew for certain. It is the same for both of us.

It was never the snowstorm that we had to worry about.

Whatever this big flurry of feelings is, that's what's keeping us locked away in this cabin. It is this—this thing swirling between us. It's not the ten feet of snow outside.

It is this delicate as a snowflake thing we both feel.

Chapter Seven

Mack

Christmas is coming and I want to celebrate it.

It's been three days now since I brought Mollie home to my cabin. It has been the best three days of my life. Even better days are coming. I never thought about a family or anything before and it might be too soon for that, but this woman has me thinking all sorts of things.

Most importantly, that I want to celebrate with her, even if it's all I get before the roads clear, and she's gone from my life. Bringing her here ruined her plans to open her shop before the holiday. I can never make up for that. What I can do is try to make it a Christmas she won't ever forget.

"We need a tree," I say casually late in the afternoon on our third day locked away together, "don't you think so?"

We're sitting by the fireplace—one she started and has kept going because she seems to enjoy the task—her wrapped up in one of my sweaters and me in just sweats. She seems to like to touch me, and I like that touch, so I indulge her however she wants.

Her eyes light up as she twists on my lap, cocking her head. Her pretty eyes search my face, as if waiting for the punchline. I mean it though and she reads me so well it barely takes a glance for her to see it. She squeals and leaps to her feet, rushing from the living room.

I watch her shapely backside, bare and a little pink from when I fucked her from behind less than an hour ago, sashay away. I adjust myself in my sweats and go to follow her. I find her in the hall off of the kitchen hastily tugging on some of my cold weather gear.

"Let's go. I need a hot lumberjack to cut down the perfect tree," she says with a wink, excitement lacing her words.

I would let Mollie order me around for the rest of my life, so I snap to it. We're dressed and out the door in less than ten minutes. None of the roads have been cleared this far up but I cleared a few walking paths last night, just in case of emergencies. I could radio into town to get my guys to clear the way faster, but I won't bother them yet.

That snowstorm gave me the perfect excuse to keep Mollie as long as I can.

"It's beautiful here," she muses as she peers out over the mountainside as we walk the narrow paths, "I see why you never want to leave."

My eyes are on her because though I love this view, I've had it a long time. I won't ever tire of the view of her. I don't know how long I'll get to have it, so I'll cherish it while I can. She reaches out to find my hand between us. As she laces our fingers together, I feel the coiling connection I've felt growing between us wind tighter around me.

"With you here I might never leave," I tease gently, but we both know I mean it. I don't have to pretend otherwise because it's obvious how I feel.

"Have you ever thought…was a family ever part of your plans?"

We stop on a landing that opens up to a wide spread of fir trees. I tug her to face me, reaching out to brush her windblown hair from her face. I should lie to her to protect us both. I should say it's not for me, because I never thought it was. But I've not lied to her yet and I won't start now.

"I can't say it ever was. My life was not built for it. Not just living up here on this mountain, either. Just how I was raised, how I lived for too long, how I ended up here. I never considered it an option for me," I keep my words gentle because already I've learned what I say and how I say it matters to her.

"What about," she takes a shaky breath, her eyes darting anxiously before they swing back to pin me down, "now? What about me?"

Dropping the ax and ropes I carry to the ground at our feet, I step into her space. My fingertips trace her beautiful face as I tip her head back. She is stunning in the sunlight, and I count the freckles on her skin, reminding myself to kiss each of them slowly when we get back to the cabin.

"Now…do you really want me to answer that, Mollie?"

"Yes, I really want to hear your answer. Would I've asked if I didn't?"

"I basically kidnapped you because I wanted you to myself. I brought you here knowing the risk of us getting stuck up here. It was selfish of me to do that. Would I do it again to get what we've had the past few days? You are goddamn right I would, and as bad as I feel about your shop, I wouldn't change a thing," I lower my voice as I touch my nose to her, speaking my next words against her mouth.

"Do I like the idea of you barefoot and pregnant in my cabin? The idea of keeping you to myself and breeding you with my child? Fuck yes, I like that idea, darlin'. Do I like the idea of driving you to town to run that shop of yours knowing the whole world would know your mine because you've got my kid inside you? Fuck, yes," I growl my words, the visions my words are conjuring up driving me crazy.

"Why would I be barefoot?" she whispers but she's teasing, and I take her mouth in a searing kiss because I adore her sassy mouth.

When we come up for air, we don't talk about how heavy our talk was. We carry on with our walk, talking about trees and my job clearing them for lumber. She asks about the business and I tell her I came in without a clue how to run it, but my heart is in the right place. I just want to keep my guys working, safely clear trees and replant as we go, and keep myself busy.

"Oh! There it is, look!" She cries as she spots a tree in the distance, rushing forward.

My chest twists as she pulls me behind her, the sight of her so excited doing funny shit to me. I would give her anything and right now, she wants this six-foot fir. That means she's getting this six-foot fir. I would level this entire clearing if she asked me to.

I quickly tie off the base of the tree and secure it to another to be sure it doesn't fall wrong. I caution her to stay behind me and get to work. It's a tall, full tree, with a healthy trunk. It takes a bit of time and plenty of axe swings, but I drop my axe and step back when it starts to go.

"Careful darlin', it's going," I call as I back up, keeping her behind me as I grab the rope at the base of the tree.

As planned, it falls forward, away from us, and crashes gently into the snow. I quickly fashion the rope around the middle and bottom, making a rope handle so we can drag it back through the snow. I turn back to her to ask if she wants anything else—because I would really cut down whatever she asked of me.

"That might be the manliest thing I've ever witnessed," she hums as she bites her lip, her eyes sliding over me as I drag the tree a few feet.

Suddenly I don't care much about trees or the snow we're knee-deep in. I barely notice the cold, in fact. Heat rushes through me as she saunters towards me. Her hand comes out, her fingers brushing through my beard the way I've grown to crave. When they trail around my neck, her nails scoring down my skin through the sweat, I hiss, yanking her against me.

"You want fucked in the snow?" I warn her as I lift her against me.

"I just might, lumberjack. God you're a beautiful man," her eyes close as I twist to pin her to a tree, "I bet no one has ever told you that because men never hear that they're beautiful. You are beautiful, Mack. Yes, I want fucked in the snow," she pleads as she starts to shake against me.

"It's cold out here, Mollie," I say even as I notch my cock between her thighs, seeking her heat, "Christ, I want to fuck you though. It smells like winter and pine trees, but I can still smell how hot your pussy is."

"Please, don't make me beg, because I will," she says it as if I wouldn't like to hear it, but God, I would.

I pull at the sweats she has on, just enough to bare her to me, and start to rub at her soaked sex. I pump my fingers into her, but she knows what she wants and it ain't my fingers. She yanks at the button and zipper on my jeans. Her warm little hands wrap around my cock and pump me slowly.

And then her hips drop as her legs loosen on my waist. Watching me, she slides down my dick slowly, her eyes fluttering as she takes me to the hilt. I settle in the warm wetness of her, my hands gripping her hips. We're both so close already it won't last long for either of us.

"Mollie," I say her name like a prayer as I start to lift her slowly, "you are beautiful. When I first saw you smile, when you laughed when I locked you into my jeep, when you came for the first time with me inside you, and right now. You are fucking beautiful and I…. oh, that's it, baby. Come on my cock, I love how good that feels," I roar as I slam her down and thrust up at the same time.

"Mack! Don't stop, don't stop, come inside me," she pants her demands, hands fisting my hair, hips twisting as she fucks me.

It is freezing out and we're surrounded by a few feet of snow on the side of the mountain. Three days ago, we were complete strangers. Now we don't feel like strangers at all—so I do as I'm told. I don't stop. Not 'til I'm jerking inside her until seed spills down her thighs.

When I pull out of her, she makes a sad little sound. It's a sound she makes every time I leave her body. If I had my way, I'd never leave that sweet heat. I go to fix her clothes but stop when I see my cum coating her slit. Using two fingers, I smear it into her velvety skin then shove some of it inside her.

I'm saying without words that I meant my statement about her being barefoot and pregnant—well, except the barefoot part.

Chapter Eight

Mollie

Watching Mack put together a Christmas tree is the sexiest thing I've ever seen. Besides watching him chop it down for us, of course.

After chopping down a tree for us to put up for Christmas, he grows excited to decorate it. Being snowed in atop a mountain makes that difficult. But whatever I ask of him, he figures out a way to make it happen. We start the day without a tree and by late afternoon, it's up and we're decorating it.

We make garlands of popcorn he pops for us and berries I pick from the bushes surrounding his cabin. Pinecones, Edison light bulbs, and more berries become ornaments. After we finish, he fixes us a plate of oatmeal raisin cookies and big mugs of milk as we sit back to survey our work.

"Well, I think it's a damn fine-looking tree," he says as he dunks his cookie in my milk and takes a big bite.

"Me too, lumberjack. Thanks for chopping it down for us."

As I praise his handiwork, I swear his chest puffs out with pride. I find it impossible that a man so sweet and good prefers life up here on this mountain all alone. He's told me over the past few days that he had a rough go of things growing up and he joined the military to escape. It was a choice he regretted but he stuck with it until he found his home here in Driftwood.

For as different as we are, we have so much in common. Our desire to have something solid and whole for ourselves first most. Though he grew up in a big city while I was raised in a small town just like Driftwood, we have a lot of the same wants and desires for our lives.

His big hand rubs at my belly beneath the sweater he let me wear and I go hot all over. Not only did he admit he thought of me pregnant with his child today, he all but tried to make that a reality. Looking in his eyes as he pushed his seed inside me with a satisfied smirk sent a confusing mix of hope and need through me.

Three days ago, we were on paths that may have never crossed. Now I can't even think of my life back in town without wondering how I'd do it without him. I feel as if this place, right here with him, is the home I've been searching for.

"What would you like most for Christmas?" he asks gently, his hand rubbing slow circles at my belly.

"Could we make some cookies together and watch Holiday Inn?"

"What you want most is to be here, with me?" he presses, clearing his throat as his hand tenses on my skin.

Panic, heat, want, doubt, all of it courses through me as we look at each other. I'm seated on his lap in his big armchair by the fire, my legs kicked up on the arm. I know what he means and until he asked, I didn't know if I had the answer. But as I answer—as scary of an answer as it is—I feel the truth of my answer down to my bones.

"I hoped to get my shop open before the storm. Mother nature has other plans. So maybe that's what I want for the new year. Right now, yes what I want for Christmas is to be here, with you," my words come out slow at first until they're rushing out with joy.

Mack is a man of few words but the words he does give me always carry weight. I like it about him mostly because I often find myself filling the spaces with words. Being up here with him, I'm slowly learning to appreciate the quiet here. When he wraps his thick arms around me and nuzzles his face into my chest, it says more than words ever could.

"You will get your shop open, darlin'. I promise you that," he kisses my neck and then gives me a squeeze that rattles my ribs.

He gave me that promise before, but I didn't take it too seriously. Now, I'm starting to think he really means everything he says. Must be why he doesn't say much at all. I don't mind the silence he gives so often. It's peaceful and so is the crackling of the fireplace, the falling snow, and the occasional meow of his stubborn cat Otto.

It is a kind of quiet I could get used to.

Back in town, I've been dealing with a different kind of quiet. One born of the locals not trusting an outsider. Mayor Bernie explained plenty of other folks tried to set up shop here too. Just to make a quick buck and bolt just as the town began to warm to them. I have no plans to profit and split.

Now that I met Mack and have been here in the cabin with him, I don't think I could leave town. I don't know what this means for either of us. I know I had a very linear plan for my fresh start—one that did not involve a man. He made it clear he never had plans for a life off this mountain.

Maybe we can find a way to both get what we want.

"If I made you a present, would that be ok?" I wonder as I comb my fingers through his thick hair.

"Only if you let me make you one," he shoots back lightning quick, kissing gently at my collar.

"Do you have something in mind?" I laugh as his beard rubs at my skin as he nuzzles into me.

"I think I can pull something together for you. Watching you put that tree together today gave me plenty of ideas. You like the holiday for the right reasons. Making moments you want to remember. That's a beautiful thing."

Tears well up in my eyes as he squeezes me tight again. Just when I think he can't get any better, he does or says something like that. He brought me here to keep me safe without even knowing me. He cut down a tree and helped me decorate it so we could have a real Christmas.

Never have I felt so connected to someone so quickly. From the moment I saw him smiling at me in town, I knew I wanted to know him. I've also never wanted someone as desperately as I want him. Once he touched me, it was as if I had never felt another touch before—and I feel as if I never want to feel another again.

Dating for me has never been a priority. I was chasing something in the city that would keep me from poverty and loneliness back home. My friends, my work, my success, and other men, nothing chased any of it away. I was always afraid of losing people, of losing what I thought I had gained, and losing myself. In the end, I lost all of it anyway.

Coming here for a fresh start, I convinced myself I had to achieve something. I had to open that store. I to partner with the townspeople to source my materials. I had to succeed here like I thought I had succeeded in the city. Months later, I don't feel as if I've achieved much of anything.

"Tell me what's in your head, darlin'?" Mack breathes his words against my ear before he kisses the lobe.

Wrapping my long hair around his hand, he tugs my head back gently. His eyes search mine as he waits for me to answer. It feels as if he can read all the parts of me, I always manage to hide. Parts I always figured were faults but that he looks at as important pieces of who I am.

"I'm thinking about my shop. About how I wound up here, wanting to even open a shop. How that wound up bringing me right here, with you," I gaze into his eyes, brushing his dark hair back as emotions wash over me.

"Whatever brought you here to Driftwood, I'm damn thankful for it. About as thankful as I am for the storm that let me keep you for a few days. I don't need you to make me a Christmas gift, Mollie. Having you here right now, for Christmas that's a hell of a gift."

His big hand cups the side of my face, his thumb drifting over my lips. Leaning into the touch, I brush my fingers through his beard, smiling when he closes his eyes and lets out a sigh.

"It feels like a gift to me too. It might just be the best Christmas ever, huh? I do want to make you something though. Besides the best oatmeal cookies, you have ever had—my mama's recipe—but I need to go forage for what I need for your gift," I insist before I peck a kiss at his lips.

"Foraging? On my mountain during a blizzard? I think not darlin'," he scoffs, kissing me hard and tightening his thick arms around me.

"I adore the sexy lumberjack thing, I really do, but just because I lived as a city girl for a minute doesn't mean I can't handle myself up here," I tease back as I try to twist from his embrace playfully.

A crackling sound cuts through our laughter and scares me silent. Before I can even ask, a man's gruff voice calls his name. He leaps to his feet, spinning to deposit me on my butt in his chair. Pressing a kiss atop my head, he bolts to the other side of the room, muttering something about answering his crew.

Always one to seize an opportunity when I see it, I dart past him and up the stairs. I want to make him a gift so that means going out on the mountain. I grab warm clothes from his closet, lingering to breathe his delicious piney scent into my lungs. Pulling on boots five sizes too big even after I pull on several pairs of socks, I try not to stomp down the stairs.

At the bottom of the stairs, I take a peek around. I frown when I don't see him anywhere. Tilting my head, I wait until I hear his voice. It's coming from behind the stairs, so I make a break for the door. Opening it, I start to step out—until I hear him chuckle and my curiosity gets the best of me.

"No, don't bother making your way up here. Doing just fine up here. Hell, it's a damn dirty thing to do to keep her up here knowing we can get back to town, I know it. I just ain't finished with her yet."

Even inside the cabin I'm frozen inside out. I can't get enough breath in my lungs to survive. Pain twists in my chest as I watch a man I thought I was falling for joke about keeping me up here until he's *finished* with me. Being up here has kept me from getting my shop open on time—something he clearly doesn't care about.

Now I can't wait to escape.

Chapter Nine

Mack

Saying out loud that I think I'm in love feels fucking good.
Now to give the words to Mollie.
Before I can do it right, I need a little more time. I want to do it on Christmas when I give her the gift I still need to make for her. I thought my plan was ruined when I got a radio call from my crew. It's still snowing pretty good, but they have cleared most of the town.

Ridge, my crew leader, let me know he could get us cleared out by tomorrow. I told him not to bother just yet. I spared him the details, but I explained that I need to buy some time with my woman. I also need to gather what I need for her gift.

Rounding the corner to tell her I changed my mind about not letting her do her own foraging, I stop in my tracks. The door is standing wide open and snow is blowing in. I see boot prints on the porch and realize she must have gone out.

Realizing not only did she go out, but she went out while I was talking to Ridge on the radio. I replay what the short conversation and dread fills me. I was boastful and cocky about finding her and falling for her. If she heard me talking with Ridge, she might have gotten the wrong idea.

"Christ woman, I knew you wouldn't give me any peace," I say to the empty cabin before I rush to the door.

Grabbing a coat and slipping on my boots, I storm from the house after her. I follow her tracks that lead down the porch and east. She can't get very far going east because to get to the road off the mountain, you have to head west. It's still early afternoon but it gets dark fast up here and it's still snowing. I have to find her fast.

I follow the tracks for half a mile, impressed she got so far so fast. I can't be sure she is not out here foraging like she mentioned but I have a sick feeling in my gut. I seem to have a talent for pissing her off—not that it doesn't turn me on to watch her get riled up.

I told Ridge I feel like a shit for bringing her up here like I did and slowing down her opening her shop up. I couldn't know what this would turn into for us, but I had an inkling that it was something different when I first loaded her up in my jeep. I've never had anything serious with a woman before, so I was clueless about this.

If I screwed this up...no, *no* I can't fuck this up.

"Mollie! We need to talk, darlin'," I shout into the whipping winds.

"No! Screw you!"

I almost laugh when I hear her shouting back but with the winds, I can't figure out where she's at. Her tracks change up on me, going in circles then fading out completely. I curse and circle back, wondering if she outsmarted me. If she realized she was going the wrong way she might have turned back.

She might have found the right way down this mountain and out of my life.

"Another storm is coming, girlie and we can't be out here in it. Whatever sent you out in a blizzard, we can talk about it back at the cabin. Let's not play games now!"

"Let's not play games? Some choice words there, buddy. You are the storm, Mack. You and your bullshit sexy lumberjack game to get a woman locked away until you're *finished* with her. Well, lumberjack, I'm finished with you!"

There she is, eyes wild, lavender hair blowing in the wind, chest pumping as she unloads on me. It's a beautiful sight, I can't lie. To know I get her worked up, that she is upset and hurt because of me, it's awful. But it's also amazing. It means she's in this as deep as I am. I can work with that.

"Oh no, we're not finished. No, no, we're just getting started. You know it; that's what's got you out here fired up like this. You are an independent woman who came to Driftwood to start your life how you wanted. I respect that, Mollie, I do. Things change, they just do," I start to go on, but she marches through the snow, poking her finger in my chest.

"*Nothing* has changed. I came here for me and my shop. Not for you, that cabin, or this mountain. None of that has changed because you fucked me good for a few days. As I said...*I am* finished with you, lumberjack."

I bite back my smirk because, God, she's stunning when she's fired up. It's not the time to enjoy her anger. I can do that later, in our bed. I realize what set her off from my talk with Ridge. I fucked up by letting my pride in having her inflate my words, so I did this. I need to fix it.

"You fucked *me* good for three days," I say her words back to her, reaching out to cup her jaw and tip her head back, "you also opened me up and made me want a life I never even thought about for you. Nothing is changed about you and your shop, sure. What has changed is you, and me, and this that we found up here."

Tears slip down her temples and it breaks my heart that I hurt her. That I let my ego do the talking. I was bragging about her and lamenting how I wasn't done having her to myself. I'm a man falling in love. I don't exactly know how to talk about it—especially with another guy about as closed off as I am. I fucked up, and I own that.

"Who do you think you are, Mack? Not someone who tells me how my life is going to go, let me answer for you. Three days ago, we were strangers, that hasn't changed. I don't know you and you sure as hell don't know me. I'm getting off this mountain—now that I know your crew cleared it—and opening my shop. We can stay strangers."

Her words carry pain and anger but it's not all because of my foolish mouth, I know that. Mollie is confused by the startling change in both of our lives. She's wrong—we aren't strangers, and it scares her that I know her better in a few days than I think she's let anyone know her before.

"You will open your shop, absolutely. I promise I'll do whatever you need to see it opens. After Christmas. My crew cleared the roads, yes. I would have told you." I wince because that's bullshit, and I don't want to have lies between us. "Hell, that's a lie. I would have kept you here as long as it took," I admit because she deserves to know the truth.

Mollie deserves to know I'm crazy about her and I'll stop at nothing to make her feel the way I do. I didn't know when I brought her up here we'd wind up here. I just couldn't walk away from her that day in town. No way in hell I can walk away now after having her.

Just like she said that first day, I'd take her home right now if she asked. If she tells me she wants to go back to town and never see me or step foot in my cabin again, well I guess I'd have to live with that. I've no clue how I'd live with it knowing how good this feels but, I'd have to.

"As long as it took for what, exactly? For you to be finished with me?"

"I won't ever be finished with you," I roar, my words echoing of the dense mountains around us.

Her big eyes get huge, and she stumbles back a bit. I go to catch her before she slips but she puts her hand out. I watch her take in my words, her chest pumping rapidly with her breaths. Her mouth opens a few times, shaky hands push through her hair, and she mutters absently. I start to ask if she has panic attacks and if I'm witnessing one.

"Say that again. I need you to make me understand. Run it by me real slow, lumberjack," her eyes narrow as she says her words low and slow.

"You heard what I said, and you know what I mean. Hell, darlin', I said the same things a hundred different ways this weekend. Too bad you heard me telling a buddy while I was bragging about you like a cocky son-of-a-bitch. I think I did it to let him know—and my whole crew—that you are mine and when they meet you next week, they better know it."

I also told Ridge the whole crew will be at her dispense to get her shop going. I was a dick for bringing her here when I did. To make it up to her, I enlisted my logging crew to do whatever she needs of them at the shop. He said he'd let the folks in town know she's here to stay so her and her shop will be welcomed with open arms. And open wallets.

Because I'm a man of few words, I needed just a few to get those points across to Ridge. While he was giving me shit for falling for a woman I just met, I was bragging about all the reasons I feel. I got cocky-- that's what she heard. She heard me making it very clear she is spoken for.

"We are *strangers*, Mack," she says in exasperation, stomping her foot.

Tired of this game she likes to play—even if it turns me on and we both know how it ends—I close the distance between us in a few feet. I scoop her up and throw her over my shoulder, just like I did the day we met. I turn to head back to the cabin, ignoring how she pounds her fists on my back and kicks. I smack her ass hard enough the crack echoes against the mountainside and she shrieks.

"You turn me on when you get sassy but it ain't safe out here. Ridge said another storm is coming and if you don't believe me," I whirl around to aim her in the direction of the thick gray skies churning behind me, "take a look. You can sass and smart off once we're home. At home I can fuck the sass out of you, just like you're asking for."

Since she didn't get far, we're back at the cabin in no time. Worried about how quiet she is, I set her gently on the porch. Taking a step back, I search her face in hopes of figuring out what she's thinking.

"What's in your head darlin'?"

Mollie is quiet but her face twists with emotions. Before I can say anything more, she takes a few steps closer. Her hand comes out, brushing over my beard as she slowly smiles. But her eyes shimmer with tears.

"You called this home. As in... *our* home. Did you mean that?"

"Hell, yes, I meant it. Could you call this *your* home, Mollie?"

Chapter Ten

Mollie

"Could you call this your home?"

Mack watches me with a softness on his handsome face that makes my chest swell with emotions. His voice is gruff, and I see everything I feel shining back at me in his eyes. He always needs just a few words to get his point across and these words mean everything.

A month ago, hell even three days ago, I'd have told him I was not going to sacrifice myself or what I wanted for him. I already lost so much. Giving up the dream I can almost touch just to be locked up here with him sounds impossible. Only somehow, I know that's not what he's asking when he asks me to make this place my home. To make this our home.

We were strangers three days ago, but it's never felt that way. From the moment we met, it felt as if we knew the things that mattered. The important things—his cabin and his crew and my shop—and things that people sometimes never learn about the people they love.

Because that's what he's asking right now. He's not asking me to be locked away in this cabin with him. He's just asking me to be here with him and make it our home. He's asking me to make his home *our home*. At least, I hope that's what he's asking.

"You want me here? With you? All the time, like...forever and ever?"

Mack seems to ponder my question for a beat before his beautiful face breaks into a smile. He nods, taking a step towards me as I take one back. He reaches out, slowly working on the zipper and buttons of my coat.

"And ever. Maybe even after that. I didn't know when I brought you here, I'd never want you to leave. But I don't. I never want you to leave. Only when you need to run the shop, will we get running. Hell, I'll take you to town if I gotta carry you, if you want to open in in time for Christmas," his voice is teasing but as he pushes my jacket off and swings the door open behind me, he sobers, "I'd do anything for you, Mollie. Anything you ask—except let you go. I don't think I can watch you leave this mountain without a promise that you're coming back home to me as soon as you can."

Boy, once he gets talking, he sure gets the words right. We're inside the cabin now and I stop pushing at our layers of clothes to look around. I do want to call this place home. I do want to make promises to him that I'll always come back home to him. And I do want to open my shop—but not before we have Christmas together.

"You may carry me to town after the new year. You promised me oatmeal raisin cookies and Holiday Inn for Christmas. I'm holding you to that, lumberjack," I say it in a raspy whisper because my throat is tight with emotion.

As he kicks the door shut behind him, he pulls the last of my clothes off. He's gloriously naked and I take a moment to enjoy the view. Again, he scoops me up, but this time he doesn't throw me over his shoulder. Cradling me in his arms, he crosses the room to the fireplace. Beside it, the tree shimmers in the late afternoon and the room smells of pine and fire.

This right here, feeling this, this is what I want most for Christmas.

Folding to the floor by the crackling fire, he spreads me out as we warm up. His big hands rub over me, at first to help warm me, before the touch changes. He cups a breast in his hand, plumping it, bending his head to suck at the nipple. Then he tugs at the budded tip until the sting of pleasure has me writhing beneath him. Chuckling, he dips his head again, kissing and nipping as his beard rubs delicious friction at my skin.

"Mack," my moan comes out throaty and needy and he bites my shoulder.

His hand slides between my legs and he starts to rub tight, hard circles at my clit. I twist my hips into the touch, greedy for the pleasure he gives me every single time. His blunt fingers spread me open then push inside me and I claw at his shoulders, shouting his name. He starts to pump those thick fingers and I see stars as I come so hard, I start shaking.

"There it is, give me that good stuff, darlin'. Christ I won't ever want to taste, touch, or be wrapped tight in anything but this pussy," he growls, rubbing hard and fast at my clit now, watching as I edge another orgasm.

"Please, I need more," I whisper as I pepper kisses down his throat.

"I'll give you more. I'll give you everything, Mollie. Come here," he gruffs, lifting me and twisting us at the same time, bringing me astride him, "slide down here and take me inside you."

He lands a slap at my ass as I shimmy on his hardness, whimpering at how thick and long it is as it slides against my slit. Pulling back, I watch as I lift up then slowly drop over him. I cry out as he fills me full, my hands flat against his chest as I take him as deep as I can.

"Oh, oh," I moan as I lam my hips down as I start to come again, the rub of him against my sweet spot sending me careening over the edge.

"Christ, that's it. Now fuck yourself on my cock. Make us both come, baby."

Whimpering, I start to move. Our eyes lock as I slowly rock at first, rubbing my swollen clit against the base of his big cock. His slides rough hands up over my hips and up to cup my tits. His palms rub at my nipples and pleasure crashes through me, wave after wave. I speed up, circling my hips in a figure eight and starting to bounce a little.

Lowering my upper body, I pant his name as I kiss him hungrily. He had it right. I won't ever be finished with him. This is too good to give up or to walk away from. He can lock me up here in his hideout if that's what he needs. I won't give this up—it feels too good.

"Yes," I chant as I bounce faster and faster, "Yes, Mack. This can be my home. *Our home.* I won't ever leave if that's what you want," I promise as I grind on his cock.

"Fuck. There it is," he growls, gripping my hips and slamming me down on his shaft.

We come together, pleasure bouncing between us like an echo on the mountain. I can feel him jerking inside me as he fills me with his sticky pleasure. He drags me down to him, kissing me roughly as I shudder against him. His lips flutter down my jaw, my neck, and my shoulder.

We lie together in the warmth of the firelight as the skies outside slowly darken. It's quiet for a long time, just the crackling of the fire and a few disgruntled sounds from Otto. It doesn't feel like we need words just yet and I know when we do, he'll get them right.

When he finally does speak, I laugh out loud because I was right.

"Can we bake the cookies tonight? You did make me chase you in the snow and then fuck you into moving in with me. Cookies seem like a fair return on the effort I exerted," he insists as we lie facing each other.

Reaching out, I brush my fingers over his beard, up his temple, and through his hair. He captures my wrist and brings my hand to his mouth, kissing the palm gently. His eyes search mine and when he speaks again, his voice is gentle but firm.

"I want you here, Mollie. I want you to open your shop and I want you to come home to me. That's what I want most for Christmas. A shot at this, with you."

"I was wrong," I say, watching his brows shoot up before I go on, "we were never really strangers, I think. Not really. You didn't need to lock me up for me to want to stay with you. Three days, three months, three years. I don't need more time to know what I want. I want this to be our home and I want to stay locked up here forever with you."

We are doing this. We're holding tight to this thing we found after two folks smiled at each other in the snow. Maybe in a month he won't want me here. Maybe in six months I'll grow tired of the cute cabin and the sexy lumberjack who built it.

Something tells me I won't have to worry about it either.

I love his mountain hideout and I think, just maybe, I love him too.

"About those cookies, darlin'," he says, rubbing his beard at my breasts and smacking my ass.

Laughing, I let him lead me to the kitchen where we find everything we need to make the best oatmeal cookies ever. While they cook, we talk about what comes next and how it will all work. He bends me over the counter and rides me hard, telling me it will work however we need it to. Eating me through two orgasms, he only stops when the timer goes off and we take a plate of the fresh cookies back to the fireplace.

We share a mug of milk as we talk about Christmas memories and devour our cookies. It's not yet Christmas but being here with this man, by a fireplace, eating cookies, and tucked snuggly in this cabin, I can't think of anything more joyful and bright.

Mack doesn't need to make me a gift—he already gave me what I wanted most for Christmas.

I was looking for a place to call my own—and I got him and his mancave—and he gave me a place I can call mine.

Epilogue

Mack

Christmas will forever be my favorite holiday now.

I'll never forget it's when I found a woman I could open more than my hideout to. When I found Mollie, I found the person who made me feel whole, who made me want to truly live, and the woman who I hope to spend the rest of my life with.

After being snowed in for four days, we do venture back to town. Not just to be sure her shop weathered the storm, but to get a few things. And to pack up the little place she'd been renting so she can make the move to my place. Before we leave town, we stop at the general store once again, because she promised me one more week locked up together on the mountain.

"But no more," she says with authority as we load the jeep up with bags, "I have a business get going and a town to win over, lumberjack."

I don't tell her both issues have been dealt with. My guys let the whole town know to be good to Mollie and even spoke to some local farmers she can source materials with. I told her I would give her everything and I meant it. I don't say words I don't mean.

Once we finish up in town, we stop at The Barn, the only bar in town, and thank the guys for their help clearing the town and the mountain roads. Whenever we don't have landings to clear, they pretty much keep to themselves or find more work to do. They never turn down hard work and doing something for a friend isn't work to them.

After she charms the boys, she insists they bring their ladies to her shop. None of them have ladies and when she finds that out, she gets a little too excited. She promises to take care of that for every one of them, even Killian who swore off relationship with any human years ago. I get her out of there before she gives them too many ideas, and we promise to see them after the New Year.

Back at the cabin, she puts things away and makes my home hers as she sings along to the little radio playing Christmas tunes. While she's occupied, I head out to my work shed to put together a gift for her. Christmas is tomorrow and I want it to be the first of many for us both.

When I finally get it right, I find a little box and some brown paper and twine. Wrapping it up as best my beat-up hands can manage, I head back in. I stop in my tracks when I find her. Besides her things and some more groceries—everything to make more cookies—she insisted on some clear tree lights for our tree.

Standing beside it, she glows in the twinkling light of our very first Christmas tree. Like I have so many times since we met, I take a moment to note every little detail. How her lavender hair looks against the big white sweater she has on. How bright her beautiful eyes look and the pretty pink flush on her cheeks. She is stunning and she is my perfect Christmas gift. I can't wait to unwrap her beneath the tree.

"Look at you," I husk as emotions choke my words and make the hand holding her gift shake.

Twirling to face me, she smiles bright and beautiful, laughing. It's the same laugh I heard that first day. The same one I want to hear for the rest of my life. It speaks to my soul like nothing else ever has and I don't think I can ever go without her. I don't know if I can give her what she needs, but I sure want to try.

"Look at *you* lumberjack," she teases with a sexy smirk, crossing the room to press her perfect body against mine.

"Got your gift," I say with pride, shaking the box a little, "I have one other gift I want to give you though."

Those bright eyes of hers shimmer in the light of the tree and her little hand passes over my zipper. I grunt and slap her ass. Yes, I want to give her some dick, but that's not what I mean. I always want to give her dick, that's a gift for me though.

"Can I unwrap it now?" she asks with a tilt of her head as she starts to undo the zipper.

Stopping her, I set her back, tucking the gift into the tree with the ornaments. It sits about perfect. Walking over to the fireplace, I set her down at the hearth. It's crackling behind her because she starts a damn good fire, and she glows in the light of it. Taking a deep breath, I kneel in front of her. I almost laugh when she gasps but, no, not just yet. Soon.

"I had no damn right to bring you up here the way I did. It cost you something, so I won't ever stop making that up to you. But I'm not sorry, Mollie. Not really, and I should be. I'm not sorry because…well, I found something better than a logging landing or a shop in Driftwood. I found you…I found love. It's been three days, and hell yes, we were strangers before. But you said it yourself—we really weren't strangers at all."

"I am a fool for you, Mollie Winters. I want you to know I'm no fool, though. I'll take care of you, be good to you, and provide for you. I'll ask you to marry me when it's not a fool's question," her gasp makes me stop but I clear my throat and go on, "I'll give you children and be the best husband and father I can be. I *will* love you, Mollie. I don't need to say the words to feel them or to know they mean something real. I don't need you to say them either, but when they come, I want to hear them as often as you feel them," I plead, reaching up to brush my thumb over her cheek as tears trickle down.

"I want to hear it too, Mack. I don't think we need to say it yet, even if with both feel it," her voice breaks but she powers through, smiling through what I hope are happy tears, "because I feel it. I want to know when we say it that we're saying it because we can't go another minute without saying it or hearing it. We have time, lumberjack. This is no longer your hideout, Mack. We're going to make it our home."

I let her unwrap her gift—but not the one I carved out in the shed.

That one she opens later, just as the sun comes up on Christmas morning. With Holiday Inn playing and fresh oatmeal cookies baked, we open the gifts we made each other. Hers is an ornament—I tell her I plan to make her one every year, to fill out tree with memories. Its just a circle of wood with my last name—Felle—carved in the middle and both our names above and below.

When I open the gift she made for me, my chest gets tight. It's a leatherbound book with parchment pages. On each page are handwritten notes and pieces of our time together pressed into them. Half of a pinecone like the ones we hung on the tree. Dried berries and pressed popcorn too. Stones from the mountain path when we went looking for our tree, and pieces of the fir tree we made love by.

One page has the recipe for her amazing oatmeal raisin cookies. Her handwriting is on every page, and it smells like her skin and has bits of all our moments so far. There are blank pages too, and she tells me those will be filled when she wants to capture the moments she loves the most.

It's a beautiful way to remember all the pieces of us falling in love. She gathered them together and sealed them up so I can always reach out and touch them.

And it's exactly what I wanted most for Christmas.

Driftwood Mountain Men Series

Mountain Man's Hideout

Mountain Man's Obsession

Mountain Man's Mix-up *(coming soon!)*

About the Author

Born and raised in the Midwest, reading and writing have always been Dee's passion. Short stories became long stories that finally, became books.

While playing grownup during the day, meaning working a job, Dee wrote her first book. When not reading or writing, which leaves less time than she's proud of, Dee loves spending her time with her furbabies, her husband and lots of movie nights.

Find Dee:

Facebook: **Author Page**

Reader Group: **Dee's Dolls**

Instagram: @ **AuthorDeeEllis**

Twitter: @ **AuthorDeeEllis**

TikTok: @AuthorDeeEllis

Goodreads: **Dee Ellis Author**

BookBub: **Author Dee Ellis**

Website: **Dee Ellis Author**

Sign up for my Newsletter

More from the Author

The Burn Series:

Let it Burn

Burn it Down

Burn for Me

Slow Burn

Crystal Cove Holidays Novella Series:

Snow Angel

Stupid Cupid

Chasing Glory

Tricky Treats

New Resolutions

Lucky Duck

Good Fridays

Father Figures

Scary Single

Having Grace

Tennessee Truckers Series:

First Run

Long Haul

Double Team

Big Rig

Good Buddy

Come Back

Driftwood Peaks Series:

Hard Wood: Driftwood Peak Series #1

Cherry Wood: Driftwood Peak Series #2

Thick Wood: Driftwood Peak Series #3

Deep Wood: Driftwood Peak Series #4

Bad Boys Worldwide:

Naughty Irish Sailor

Naughty British Boss

Naughty Italian Fighter

Naughty French Nerd

Naughty Arabian Prince

Naughty Scottish Rogue

Fellow Falls Trilogy:

Ride a Cowboy

Ride a Stud

Ride a Stallion

Pine Grove Passions Series:

80s Baby's:

When I Think of You

Hurts So Good

Hot For Teacher

Harmony Hollow Hawks Series

End Game

False Start

First Down

Standalones:

Mustang Maverick

Trick or Eat

Naughty & Nice

Mountain Man's Major Obsession

Work Wife

Miss Matched

Wicked Wishes

Merry Christ-Mess

Sleigh Bell Baby

Lucky Chance

Hot Lumberjack Lovin' Summer

Daddy FlyBoy

His Red Delicious

Toil & Trouble

Holi-Date

Texas Twister

Flirt Club Series:

Santa's Baby

Resolution: Double Dare

Dear Sexy Swimmer

Mr. Pink

Spring Break Heartache

His Sun Drop

Always a Bridesmaid

Her Captain's Deck

Mistletoe Magic

Hard Packed

Billionaire X2

His Cheeky Chantilly

Mountain Mancave

Shore Thing

Forgot & Found

Hard Fit

Walking Their Plank

Snowed In with The Lumberjack

Mile High Maid

Made in the USA
Monee, IL
11 February 2025